Tiny Dinosaurs

For all the Daisys. JS

OXFORD
UNIVERSITY PRESS

Great Clarendon Street, Oxford OX2 6DP
Oxford University Press is a department of the University of Oxford.
It furthers the University's objective of excellence in research, scholarship,
and education by publishing worldwide. Oxford is a registered trade mark of
Oxford University Press in the UK and in certain other countries

British Library Cataloguing in Publication Data

Data available

ISBN: 978-0-19-274454-8 (paperback)
ISBN: 978-0-19-274455-5 (eBook)

1 3 5 7 9 10 8 6 4 2

Printed in China

Paper used in the production of this book is a natural,
recyclable product made from wood grown in sustainable forests.
The manufacturing process conforms to the environmental
regulations of the country of origin.

Tiny Dinosaurs

Joel Stewart

From the creator of *The Adventures of Abney & Teal*

OXFORD
UNIVERSITY PRESS

Hi, I'm Rex, and this is my best friend Daisy.
Daisy is wild about dinosaurs!

She has dinosaur pyjamas,
and dinosaur slippers.

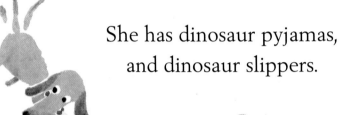

And a dinosaur toy that roars.

ROAARR!

And a dinosaur tail.

Daisy loves to read books all about dinosaurs too.

But, best of all . . .

. . . she loves playing the dino dress-up game!

Sometimes I'm a stegosaurus with bony plates down my back.

Sometimes a diplodocus
stretching for a treat.

A triceratops with
three fantastic horns.

Or a tyrannosaurus rex with fearsome teeth.

I can even be a flying reptile with great big wings!

Daisy's books say that dinosaurs
are from a long time ago.
And that there aren't any left
except for bones in museums.

'But I think there are some dinosaurs left,' whispers Daisy.
'People just haven't been looking hard enough.'

So everywhere we go,
we keep an eye out for dinosaurs.

We look up high . . .

. . . we look down low.

We look far away.

We look nearby.

And then, right at the bottom of our garden . . .

. . . we discover dinosaurs!

These dinosaurs are a lot smaller than I was expecting.
But I suppose they are just the right size for Daisy.

There is a mini stegosaurus
with plates all down its back.

A dinky diplodocus
with a stretchy neck.

A tiny triceratops
with three tiny horns.

And a noisy little t-rex.

ROAAAR!

SQUEEEK!

I'm sure that Daisy doesn't need me anymore,
not now she has real dinosaurs to play with.

So I pack my things and leave . . .

Daisy was my best and only friend in the whole world.

And everywhere I go reminds me of her.

But she won't even have noticed that I've gone.

At last I arrive at our favourite spot,
and I'm thinking how I'll be alone forever . . .

When suddenly . . .

Over the hill come five tiny dinosaurs . . .

. . . and DAISY!

'My Rex!' she shouts.
'I found you!'

Daisy did notice I was gone, after all!

'We all missed you, Rex,' says Daisy.

'I got a bit excited with the dino-games,
but nothing is the same without you.

'It's tricky when things change,
but maybe if we all try hard
things won't seem quite so bad.'

Daisy is right. It can be tricky when things change.

Like the time I got a scary new bed.

But it was okay in the end.

Or the time the cat moved in next door.

But it was okay in the end.

And the time we discovered
the tiny dinosaurs.
And maybe that will be
okay in the end, too.

'Because no matter what,'
says Daisy, 'you'll always
be my friend.

'And the tiny dinosaurs
are friendly. Come
home and you'll see.'

It *is* really good to be home.

We all wag our tails.

We roar for joy.

The tiny dinosaurs are quite silly.
(Perhaps tiny triceratops will make
friends with the dino-slippers one day.)

But we're all very
pleased to hang
around with Daisy.

In fact . . .

. . . we're all best friends together . . .

. . . good night, everyone!